THE GOLDEN ARMOUR

TRILLION
THE THREE-HEADED
LION

With special thanks to Allan Frewin

For Harvey

www.beastquest.co.uk

ORCHARD BOOKS
338 Euston Road, London NW1 3BH
Orchard Books Australia
Level 17/207 Kent St, Sydney, NSW 2000

A Paperback Original
First published in Great Britain in 2008

Beast Quest is a registered trademark of Beast Quest Limited
Series created by Working Partners Limited, London

Text © Beast Quest Limited 2009
Cover illustration © David Wyatt 2008
Inside illustrations © Orchard Books 2008

A CIP catalogue record for this book is available
from the British Library.

ISBN 978 1 84616 993 9

15
Printed in Great Britain by J. F. Print Ltd, Sparkford.

The paper and board used in this paperback are natural recyclable
products made from wood grown in sustainable forests. The
manufacturing processes conform to the environmental regulations
of the country of origin.

Orchard Books is a division of Hachette Children's Books,
an Hachette UK company.

www.hachette.co.uk

TRILLION
THE
THREE-HEADED
LION

BY ADAM BLADE

ORCHARD BOOKS

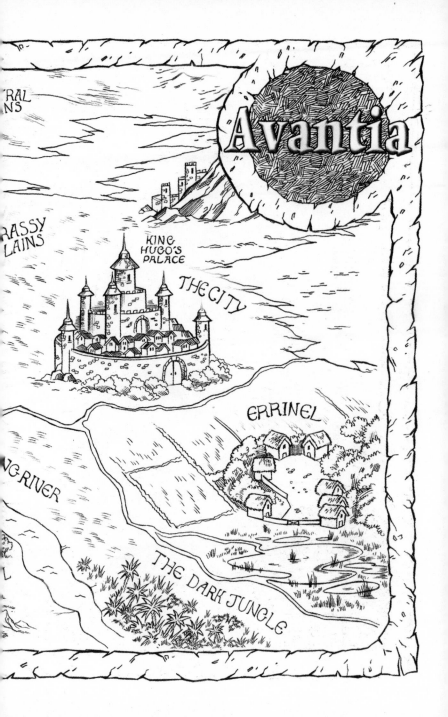

Did you think it was over?

Did you think I would accept defeat, and disappear?

No! That can never be. I am Malvel, the Dark Wizard who strikes fear into the hearts of the people of Avantia. I still have much more to show this kingdom, and one boy in particular – Tom.

The young hero liberated the six Beasts of Avantia from my curse. But his fight is far from over. Let us see how he fares with a new Quest, one that will surely crush him and his companion, Elenna.

Avantia's Beasts had good hearts that I corrupted for my own wicked purpose. Now, thanks to Tom, they are free to protect the kingdom once more. But I have created six new supreme Beasts whose hearts are evil and so cannot be set free: monster squid, giant monkey, stone charmer, snake man, king of spiders and three-headed lion. Each one guards a piece of the most precious relic of Avantia, which I have stolen: the suit of golden armour that gives magical strengths to its rightful owner. I will stop at nothing to prevent Tom collecting the complete suit and defeating me again. This time he will not win!

Malvel

PROLOGUE

The sun was setting over the central plains of Avantia. Tagus the horseman, good Beast and protector of the land, nodded his head contentedly. All was peaceful, as it had been ever since Tom had freed him from the evil curse of Malvel the Dark Wizard.

It was time to rest. Tagus stamped a heavy hoof and turned to look at the cattle in the distance. A strange shape had appeared on an outcrop of rock on the far horizon, the sun behind it. Some kind of large animal was watching the herd.

A predator!

Tagus trotted forwards warily, keeping to the cover of rocks and trees as he approached the creature. At last he was close enough to see clearly.

It was a huge three-headed lion, the sunlight shining on its thick golden fur and the shaggy manes that hung from its three heads. Six eyes burned with a wicked emerald light as it gazed down at the cattle, and its lips were drawn back to reveal fearsome, slavering teeth.

Tagus knew immediately that this was an evil Beast, sent by Malvel to cause mayhem. Instinct told him that he must confront the lion and do all in his power to destroy it. He eyed its huge paws, each one the size of his own head and studded with long, razor-sharp claws. Then, with a fierce cry, he galloped out of cover, drawing his sword as he pounded towards the lion.

The three heads turned and the three mouths bellowed with anger and hatred. The lion pounced from its position on the rock, filling the whole sky as it came crashing down on Tagus. The horse-man's sword spun from his hand as the two mighty Beasts rolled across the ground.

Tagus fought hard, kicking with his hooves and gripping one of the lion's three throats. But the two other heads came snapping at him and he could smell the Beast's foul breath as three sets of teeth sought to tear the flesh from his bones.

A powerful double blow from the horse-man's back legs sent the lion sprawling. Panting, Tagus got to his feet, but the evil Beast attacked again, jaws snapping, and its terrible weight held him to the ground. Tagus had never known such strength and savagery before. He could feel deep wounds on his flanks and neck, and sensed his death was near. The lion pinned him down, its back arching as the three heads lifted and let out deafening, triumphant roars.

Tagus struggled valiantly, but he was already too weak to break free. The heads bent down now, hungry eyes glowing, jaws snapping and ready to sink into Tagus's flesh...

Suddenly an arrow came shooting

out of nowhere, the sharp point
sinking deep into one of the
lion's paws.

The monster let out a roar of anger
and leapt back, his great body
trembling with rage. Tagus tried to get
up, but he was too badly wounded.

While one lion head tore at the
arrow, the other two were turning,
their blazing eyes searching for the
archer. A second arrow hissed,
narrowly missing one of the heads.

With an ear-splitting roar, the lion
took off, bounding away towards the
darkening plains.

Gasping with relief, Tagus looked up.

Two familiar shapes stood on the
high horizon: a boy whose golden
armour shone in the light of the
setting sun, and a girl with another
arrow already fitted to her bow.
A horse and a wolf stood poised on
the rocky outcrop behind them.

CHAPTER ONE

THE WOUNDED BEAST

"Tagus is hurt!" Tom cried, scrambling onto his horse. "Quickly, Storm!"

Elenna leapt up behind Tom. The black stallion neighed and reared, his hooves striking the air, before he set off at a gallop. Tom and Elenna clung grimly to his back, with Elenna's loyal wolf Silver close behind.

They came down off the stony crag and sped across the plains to where the injured horse-man lay. Tagus was still struggling to get to his feet, but his battle with the monstrous three-headed lion had left him weak and helpless.

Tom peered into the distance, but the evil Beast had fled, leaving no trace. There would be time enough to deal with Malvel's monster later. Right now they had to help Tagus.

"That lion would have killed him if it wasn't for your arrows," Tom shouted to Elenna as they galloped along.

"It has to be one of Malvel's evil Beasts," Elenna replied, concern in her voice. "Do you think it's the guardian of the golden boots?"

"It must be," Tom said. "This is

Malvel's final challenge – and when we win, I will have every piece of the missing armour."

The magical golden armour, the most precious relic in the kingdom, had been scattered throughout Avantia by the Dark Wizard, each piece watched over by a fearsome Beast under Malvel's thrall. So far, Tom had defeated five Beasts and collected the helmet, chainmail, breastplate, gauntlets and leg armour. Each piece had given him new powers. Now only the boots were missing.

But Malvel had held back his most deadly Beast until last! The huge, savage creature had defeated Tagus – how could he and Elenna stand up to such a monster, even with the help of his magical shield and the golden armour he had won?

Tom gritted his teeth. Whatever the outcome, he would find the evil Beast and do battle with it. All of Avantia depended on him.

They came to where Tagus was lying. The foul, musky scent of the three-headed lion hung thickly in the air. The two friends leapt down from Storm's back and ran to Tagus. His wounds were deep and bloody, showing the dreadful marks of claws and razor-sharp fangs.

"Careful!" Tom said as Tagus fought to get to his feet. "We'll help you. Slowly, now!" The Beast could not understand human speech, but Tagus would know that they meant to help.

Tom and Elenna did their best to support the horse-man as he struggled to stand. Storm came close, whinnying gently and bowing his head so that Tagus could hold on and pull himself up.

At last the wounded horse-man was upright, his arm across Storm's neck, the stallion pressing close so that Tagus would not fall. Silver prowled around them, his sharp eyes alert for danger.

"He needs to rest and recover," Elenna said. "But he won't be able to travel far." She looked at Tom. "What should we do?"

Tom pointed back towards the outcrop. The rock-face curved inwards, forming a natural shelter.

"If we can get him there, he should be hidden from danger while we deal with the lion," Tom said. He turned to the horse-man. "Come with us," he said, pointing to the outcrop. "You'll be safe there."

Tagus nodded, his face twisted with

pain. Very slowly, and with Storm at his side, he began to limp forwards.

Tom and Elenna walked at Tagus's other side, ready to help if the good Beast faltered.

"He's badly hurt," Elenna said in a low voice. "He won't be able to help us against the lion."

Tom nodded grimly. In their Quest for the golden armour they had been aided by the good Beasts of Avantia,

but it seemed that this final test would have to be completed alone.

Then the sound of cruel laughter echoed across the plains.

"Malvel!" Tom gasped, his fingers closing on the hilt of his sword.

A dark swirl, like a small whirlwind, appeared in the sky. When it had cleared, the Dark Wizard was standing in front of them, his eyes flashing.

Tom drew his blade.

"Don't try to strike me," Malvel
sneered. "You know you can do me no
harm!" He laughed again and stretched
out a hand towards them, his long, thin
fingers like claws. "You are doomed.

Your Quest is at an end! Tagus will die and you will fall to the power of Trillion – the most savage and deadly Beast you have ever encountered!"

"We're not scared of you or the Beasts you keep under your spells!" Elenna shouted. "You're the one who should be scared!"

"I?" Malvel laughed. "Scared of *you*? No, child, I feel no fear. But fear is coming for you – can you not hear it? Padding this way on four mighty paws? Listen carefully now..."

"You're a coward!" Tom shouted.

Malvel's face twisted with rage. "I will make one oath to you, boy," he spat. "I promise you pain and destruction if you dare to fight Trillion. He is more dangerous than you could ever imagine!" His eyes glowed. "And when you lie dying,

I will be there – and my face will be the last thing you will ever see!"

Then the dark whirlwind disappeared again, while the sky shook with the awful noise of the wizard's laughter.

Malvel was gone.

Tom turned to Elenna. "Aduro wasn't with him this time," he said.

Previously, Malvel had shown them horrible visions of their friend and adviser, the good wizard Aduro, bound and helpless above a pit of boiling tar. Tom knew that the only way to save Aduro was by collecting each piece of the golden armour and finishing the Quest.

"What do you think that means?" Elenna asked. "Has Malvel done something terrible to him?"

"I don't know," Tom replied, a fierce determination in his voice. "But when this Quest is over, I will make Malvel pay for all his wickedness."

He gazed at the plains. Somewhere out there Trillion was guarding the golden boots. Tom raised his sword to the sky.

"Whatever it takes!" he called out. "I will find you, Trillion! I will complete my Quest!"

CHAPTER TWO

WILD ATTACK!

Tagus let out a groan. He lay on the ground underneath the outcrop, his great chest heaving and a trail of blood trickling from the corner of his mouth.

"I really think he's dying," Elenna whispered. "Tom – what can we do?"

"I have an idea," Tom said. He pulled his shield off his back. Embedded in the wood were six magical tokens from his early Quests.

"The talon from Epos the flame bird heals all wounds," he reminded Elenna as he pulled the talon from its place in the shield. "It should help."

He knelt at Tagus's side and touched the talon against one of the Beast's deep cuts. A sudden surge of energy filled his hand and shot up his arm, making his skin tingle, and the talon began to glow red.

"It's working!" Elenna gasped.

"I think it is," Tom agreed with a smile. He lifted the talon away. The wound had closed, hardly leaving a scar. "But there are so many injuries," he murmured. "I wonder if the token will have enough power to heal them all?"

He put the talon to another wound. Again he felt the tingling sensation and again the red light surged. Hope ignited within him – soon Tagus would be well again!

But when he tried to heal the third wound, the tingling was faint and the light barely gleamed. Tom lifted the talon away. The wound had closed, but it hadn't completely healed.

Tom touched a fourth wound. The light from the talon flickered for a moment – and then it was gone.

"Why isn't it working?" Elenna asked.

"I think it needs time to fill with power again," Tom said. He looked anxiously at her. "At least, I hope that's all it is." He frowned. "But it might take hours or days for all we know. And we don't have that kind of time!" He stood up, gripping the talon. "We have to act against Trillion now," he said. "The evil Beast can't be allowed to ravage the countryside."

Tom pointed to the top of the rock that was sheltering them. "That's a good vantage point," he said. "I should be able to see Trillion if he's anywhere nearby."

"I'll come with you," Elenna said. "Storm and Silver can stay with Tagus."

Tom nodded. He and Elenna said a quick farewell to their two companions, then began the steep climb to the summit of the outcrop.

The sun had almost set by the time they stood on the high rock. Tom lowered the visor of his golden helmet, which gave him brilliant vision.

Now Tom could see the three-headed lion as clearly as if the Beast had been a sword's length away.

Trillion was causing havoc in

a herd of wild goats, leaping upon
the terrified, fleeing creatures. The
poor animals were snapped up in
the lion's three jaws then flung away.

"He's toying with them!" Tom said

angrily, his heart burning. "We'll put a stop to his game!"

But Elenna snatched at his arm. "Look!"

Tom followed the line of her eyes. A wide ring of small dark shapes was moving purposefully in their direction.

"Hyenas!" he gasped. There were twenty or thirty of them, slinking towards Tagus, Storm and Silver, their eyes shining with a hungry light.

"They must have smelled Tagus's blood," Tom said.

"Will Storm and Silver be able to fight them off?" Elenna asked anxiously.

"I don't think so," Tom said. "There are too many of them. We have to get back down there."

A drawn-out howl sounded from one of the hyenas, and then the entire pack came forward at a run, screeching and yowling as they closed in on the helpless Beast and his two animal protectors...

CHAPTER THREE

COURAGE AND STRENGTH

"We're coming!" Tom shouted as he and Elenna scrambled back down the rock-face.

But the hyenas were closing in fast, their howling echoing across the plains.

"I left my bow and arrows down there," Elenna cried.

Tom held out his shield. "Use this to defend yourself while you get them."

"But you'll need it!" Elenna gasped.

"I have other protection," Tom replied, his hand pressing against his chainmail and shining breastplate. The moment his hand touched the golden armour, he felt the magic working. The chainmail filled his heart with blazing courage. At the same time, strength flowed from the breastplate to all his muscles.

He felt no fear now. A thousand hyenas could attack – he would defeat them! He pressed the shield into Elenna's arms and leapt from the rock with a shout, his sword flashing in his hand.

He landed among the hyenas, his blade slicing the air, his other arm raised to fend off the gnashing teeth and scrabbling claws. A few hyenas fell and the others drew back, surrounding him, glaring at him, but keeping out of his sword's reach.

He saw Elenna leap down off the rock, the shield held out in front of her. A hyena pounced, but she struck

it with the shield and sent it tumbling.

"You won't defeat me!" Elenna cried out to the vicious animals. Another hyena came at her, but she side-stepped and kicked out at the creature as it plunged past her.

Storm and Silver were also fighting hard, battling to keep the hyenas away from Tagus. Storm was rearing, beating the hyenas back with his kicking hooves, the power of his legs sending the wild animals spinning through the air. The horse-man was trying to get to his feet, but Tom could see he was weak from loss of blood and could do nothing to help.

Silver was on the ground, wrestling wildly with two of the hyenas. For a dreadful moment one of them managed to clamp its jaws on the wolf's neck, but Silver quickly struggled to his

feet, shaking off his attacker.

Swinging his sword, Tom ran forwards. "Storm! To me!" he shouted.

The noble stallion neighed loudly at the sound of his voice and came plunging towards him through the mass of hyenas, hooves stamping.

Tom swung up into the saddle, grasping the reins and urging Storm towards the wolf and the horse-man. His blade flashed and spun, the golden gauntlets bestowing special sword skills. The cowardly hyenas backed away, snarling and slavering, as Tom reached Silver. A moment later Elenna was at his side, her bowstring thrumming as she shot arrow after arrow into the pack.

"Get away!" Tom shouted.

A long, whining howl of defeat sounded. The pack slunk back, then

turned and fled. Filled with joy, Tom dug his heels into Storm's flanks, urging the horse to gallop after them. He wasn't going to let the hyenas regroup and attack again – he would give them such a chase that they would never come back!

Elenna shouted, "Tom, be careful!"

But he had no fear as he galloped across the plains.

Suddenly a howl sounded from the rocks on one side. He turned his head and saw a huge hyena standing above him. Then there was another howl – from the other side. He turned his head again, and saw the shapes of more hyenas.

Two new packs had arrived!

Storm whinnied uneasily, turning about as the packs swarmed closer. They began to howl and whine again, and this time there was a new hunger in their eyes.

Tom raised his sword as the hyenas pounced.

CHAPTER FOUR

THE TALON
OF EPOS

A roar sounded in the gathering twilight, a roar so loud that it shook the air. The high-pitched baying of the hyenas was silenced.

Tom twisted in the saddle.

Tagus was approaching! The horseman had come to save him!

The good Beast was bloodied and his hide was criss-crossed with cuts, but he was standing tall and majestic again, his head held high, his great hooves stamping and his sword in his fist.

A few hyenas threw themselves at the horse-man, but his whirling sword slashed through the air like a scythe as he thundered into the pack and scattered the animals.

"Tagus!" Tom shouted in joy, brandishing his own sword.

The hyenas turned tail, racing into the gathering gloom.

Tom rode up to the horse-man. "You made it just in time," he said, hoping the Beast would understand what he was trying to say.

Tagus nodded his huge head and there was a proud light in his eyes. But he was panting and his efforts had opened his wounds again, so that drops of blood splashed onto the ground.

As Elenna and Silver came running up, Tagus staggered, his legs giving way beneath him. Tom let out a cry of concern as the good Beast fell to the ground.

"It was too much for him," said Elenna, resting her hand gently on Tagus's neck.

"He used all his strength to save us," Tom said anxiously, swinging down from the saddle and running to Tagus's side. "Elenna – give me the shield, please. Maybe Epos's talon will work again now."

Tagus lay quite still, breathing heavily, his eyes half-closed as Tom placed the talon against the worst of the wounds. The tingle ran up his arm and the red light glowed. "It's working!" Tom cried in relief.

While Tom concentrated on the next wound, Elenna gathered moss to clean the worst of Tagus's injuries and to soak up the blood. Storm whinnied softly, touching his velvet muzzle comfortingly to the side of the horse-man's face. Even Silver came and curled up at the Beast's side to keep Tagus warm as the night approached.

"How long will the talon work for?" asked Elenna.

Tom looked up at her. "Long enough
to save him from dying, I hope," he
said. A few wounds had been healed,
but there were so many more.

"The talon only has the power to
heal a few wounds at a time," Elenna
pointed out. "It might take all night."

"Then we *will* take all night," Tom
said firmly. "I'm not leaving him like

this, not after what he just did for us. Besides, I think we should rest after our fight with the hyenas. We'll need all our wits and strength before we try to tackle Trillion."

A roar sounded in the distance. Tom looked up. The three-headed lion stood on a hilltop, silhouetted against the rising moon.

"Why doesn't he attack?" Elenna asked.

"He's hoping to lure us into chasing him in the darkness," Tom said, his eyes narrowing. "He has probably set a trap for us."

At that moment, Trillion leapt down from the hilltop and vanished into the night.

Elenna stared after him. "By morning, he could be a long way away from here," she exclaimed.

"We could lose him!"

"He won't get away," Tom declared. "I'll use Aduro's enchanted map. That will guide us to him." He drew out the rolled-up parchment map from Storm's saddlebag and flung it open.

Tom had been given the magical map of Avantia at the very beginning of his Quest. Rolled up, it seemed to be an ordinary map, but when it was unrolled something extraordinary happened – it turned into a tiny living version of the kingdom. The map had always shown Tom the path to the next Beast.

Tom and Elenna stared at the map and waited. But there was no sign of Trillion on the miniature parchment plains.

"How can we fight a Beast we can't even find?" Elenna asked.

"I don't know," Tom said. "But

there *has* to be a way!"

Just then Silver got up and began to bark. He trotted away from them, his nose to the ground. Then he turned and came back to Tom and Elenna, barking again and nudging his grey head against Tom's arm. The moonlight reflected brightly in his eager eyes.

"What is it, boy?" Tom asked.

Silver sniffed again and pawed the ground, looking at Tom and Elenna, then staring off into the distance.

A smile broke over Elenna's face. "He's telling us we don't need the map," she said. "He'll use his nose to track Trillion down." She grinned at Tom. "A wolf can do more than just fight!"

"Well done, Silver!" said Tom. "We'll stay here with Tagus overnight, and first thing in the morning you can lead us to Trillion." He patted the wolf's thick fur. "I *will* defeat him, and then the golden armour will be complete!"

CHAPTER FIVE

HUNTER AND PREY

The sun had just started to rise over the hills the next morning when Silver leapt onto a rock and sniffed the air. He let out a growl and bounded away. Tom and Elenna bid a quick farewell to Tagus, then Tom jumped into Storm's saddle, reaching down to help Elenna climb up behind him.

Storm took off after the racing wolf, Tom and Elenna clinging to his back.

"From the way Silver is behaving, I don't think Trillion can be very far away," Elenna said as they galloped over the plains.

"He isn't!" Tom said. "Can't you smell him?" The foul stench of the three-headed Beast filled the air. Then the wind changed direction and Tom lost the scent. But Silver's sensitive wolf nose did not let them down. His muzzle to the ground, his tail waving high in the air, he led them towards a distant ridge.

As they approached the top, Silver paused.

"I think he wants us to hold back," Elenna said.

They waited while the wolf crept to the crest. Keeping low, he peered over, then came loping back, his tongue lolling and his eyes filled with triumph.

"I think Trillion is just beyond the ridge," Elenna whispered. "Well done, Silver!"

Tom and Elenna dismounted and crawled up to the crest. They found themselves looking down into a wide forested valley. At its bottom was a lake of still water that glimmered in the sunlight.

Tall fir trees grew right up to the water's edge, but in one place there was a clearing. Trillion was pacing slowly along the shore. A thrill of excitement ran through Tom. There could only be one reason why Trillion was here – the golden boots! The Quest was almost over, though he knew it would take all his courage and cunning to defeat the Beast.

"He's so big," Elenna murmured. "Tom, how will we ever beat him?"

Tom frowned. Elenna was right – the monster was huge, its fur shining golden in the sun, its eyes glittering emerald-bright.

"He must have a weak spot," he said, and lowered his visor, so that he could study every detail of the giant lion. As Tom watched, a bird

came swooping low over the water and Trillion lunged towards it, teeth bared and one paw swiping. The bird gave a cry of alarm and rocketed up into the sky. But Tom noticed that Trillion's other paw came close to the water's edge and that the evil Beast quickly drew back with a snarl, as if he feared or disliked the water.

"I've heard stories that lions are

afraid of water," Tom said. "They aren't good swimmers, because their manes get waterlogged and drag them down."

"And Trillion has three manes," Elenna said excitedly. "If we can lure him into the lake, we might be able to defeat him!"

Tom watched the lion, a plan forming in his mind.

"Storm isn't afraid of water," he said. "He's swum rivers with me on his back. If we could get him to go down to the lakeside to drink, I'm sure he would lure the lion."

Elenna stared at him with wide, frightened eyes. "You can't mean it!" she gasped. "Trillion could kill Storm with one bite!"

"I know," Tom admitted. "It's dangerous, but I can't think of any

other way to take Trillion by surprise."
He looked back to where the stallion
stood waiting. "Storm is clever," he
said. "When he sees the lion coming
for him, he will leap into the water
and swim to safety. We'll wait in
hiding nearby. As soon as the lion gets
to the water's edge, you can fire
arrows at him. I'll attack with my
sword, and with luck we'll force him
into the lake."

"And if we don't have any luck?"
Elenna murmured.

"Then I will do everything in my
power to see that Storm does not
come to harm," Tom vowed.

"You're right," Elenna said. "What
other choice is there?"

They found a low place in the ridge
and made their way down through
the trees, moving silently. Tom led

Storm, keeping close to him, rubbing his face against the animal's neck.

"I wish I could spare you this danger," he said to the black stallion.

Storm whinnied softly, almost as if he knew what Tom was going to ask him to do. Tom wondered if his lost father, Taladon the Swift, had ever had to make such a heart-wrenching decision.

At last they came down to where the trees met the lake's edge. Trillion's clearing was to their left. Tom peered through the trees. The lion had left the clearing, but Tom thought he saw a glimpse of tawny fur at the far edge of the open space.

Tom stroked Storm's neck. "Go, boy," he said. "Have a drink." Although he knew Storm couldn't understand his words, he added,

"The moment you see the lion, jump into the water and swim away as fast as you can. We'll do the rest."

Storm pressed his muzzle into Tom's neck.

As the brave horse walked out of the cover of the trees and went down to the edge of the lake, Tom drew his sword and Elenna fitted an arrow to her bow.

"We may be too far away here," Tom said. "Follow me." He led Elenna and Silver to a place close to the middle of the clearing. Now they were in a much better position to attack the lion.

Tom stared into the trees, carefully keeping watch on the last place he thought he had seen Trillion. He could see no sign of the Beast now – but he was sure the lion must be lurking nearby.

The foul smell still filled the air.

Storm lowered his head and began to drink. Tom's heart was thumping. He mustn't let anything happen to his horse.

Still the lion did not come. Where was Trillion?

"Oh, no!" Elenna gasped. "Look!"

Tom turned at the sound of her voice, and his heart leapt into his mouth.

Trillion was on the *other* side of the clearing! He must have gone right around the lake under cover of the trees, and was coming at Storm from behind! The evil Beast slunk silently out of the wood, his body low to the ground, his eyes fixed on Tom's black stallion.

A terrible panic gripped Tom. Storm was too far away for them to reach him in time! And he couldn't call out to warn the horse because that would let Trillion know where they were.

The plan had gone horribly wrong. Tom's faithful steed would have to pay with his life!

CHAPTER SIX

DESPERATE DANGER!

Tom scrambled to his feet, but Elenna snatched at his arm and pulled him down again.

"It's too late. Trillion will see you!" she hissed. "Keep under the cover of the trees, make your way behind him – then attack. As soon as you make your move, I'll start shooting arrows."

Tom nodded. "Good thinking," he said. But there was so little time. He could see that Trillion was getting terribly close to Storm, and still the horse had not heard him.

Tom slid quietly along the edge of the forest until he was behind the great three-headed lion. He could see the monster's huge paw prints in the soft earth – each as large as Tom's shield. Trillion was certainly the most dangerous Beast he had ever faced. But Tom had to be brave. He took a step out into the open, although even the courage bestowed by the chainmail was barely enough. He raised his arm to give Elenna the signal to begin firing her arrows.

As the first arrow bit into the Beast's shoulder, Trillion let out a fearsome roar from all three of his massive jaws, an ear-splitting noise that sent birds wheeling into the sky. Storm's head jerked up and he rolled his eyes in fear, rearing back from the huge Beast. But instead of leaping forwards into the safety of the lake, Storm bolted for the trees.

"No, Storm!" Tom shouted. "Not that way!"

Trillion was too quick for the horse. Ignoring the arrow that jutted from his thick hide, the lion pounced, blocking Storm's escape route. Tom saw his friend rear up in panic, froth gathering at the corners of his mouth.

Storm turned on his hind legs and raced for the lake, but in three great bounds Trillion was between the horse and the water, wicked eyes glinting and jaws gaping as he snarled and pawed the ground. It seemed to

Tom that the Beast was enjoying tormenting Storm – as if killing Tom's horse would be a special pleasure.

Trillion raised a paw, claws extended, ready to deliver the killing blow. But a second arrow flew from the forest. It struck Trillion in the hindquarters and hung there, quivering. Tom saw Elenna step out of the trees, already fitting the next arrow to her bow. The lion gave another angry roar. Elenna fired again. The arrow hissed through the air, catching in one of Trillion's manes. Another struck him, and then another – but they didn't seem to be injuring the lion at all. Tom realised that the Beast's hide must be too thick for the arrows to penetrate.

Storm was standing his ground even though he was terrified. Tom

knew that once the horse ran,
Trillion would bring him down.

He had to act fast. It was time to
break his cover – to rescue Storm
and defeat Trillion.

Another arrow came arcing out of
the trees. But this time flames were
crackling around its point! Elenna
must have tied dry grasses around
the arrow-head then used flint and
tinder to ignite it.

"Yes!" Tom whispered to himself. "Good idea, Elenna."

The arrow embedded itself in Trillion's foreleg, the flames searing the Beast's hair and burning its skin. Trillion let out a roar of pain, twisting and turning as he tried to quench the flames.

Tom ran forwards, quickly covering the open ground between himself and Storm, his golden leg armour giving him the extra speed that he needed. He was nearly there! Trillion was pulling the arrow from his flesh with his teeth, ignoring the flames. But the Beast froze when he saw Tom grab Storm's leather reins.

Another deafening roar blasted out from Trillion's three gaping mouths. Storm bolted, heading towards the water, with Tom clinging to his reins.

The golden armour clattered as he was dragged along and his sword fell from his fingers.

Tom lost his grip when Storm plunged into the lake. The water closed over his head and flooded his mouth. The golden armour was dragging him down!

Tom kicked hard with his feet and hauled himself up to the surface, coughing and spluttering. If it hadn't been for the protection of Sepron the sea serpent's tooth on his shield, he would certainly have drowned.

Trillion was now at the lake's edge. The Beast didn't dare come into the water but reached out a giant paw towards Storm. His fearsome claws caught Storm's saddle. With one swift movement, the stallion was plucked from the lake and sent rolling onto the ground, his long legs kicking in the air.

More arrows flew from the forest. But they were no help. Tom had to get back to his horse! He swam towards the shore, kicking fiercely to stay afloat. He grabbed hold of some reeds and heaved himself onto dry land. Struggling to his feet, he ran towards Storm. But he was too late. Trillion leapt at the horse, his claws glinting in the sun.

Then, with a sudden shock, Tom saw the sunlight reflecting off something else – the golden boots! They were lying half-hidden in the long grass, close to the fallen stallion.

As Trillion came plunging down, Tom realised that the Beast was going to crush both Storm and the magical boots.

After all the effort and danger of Tom's Quest, would the golden armour never be complete again?

CHAPTER SEVEN

THE LION'S BREATH

At the last possible moment Storm
managed to roll clear of Trillion. His
kicking legs struck the golden boots
with a clang and sent them spinning
to safety. The huge lion crashed to
the ground, tumbling over and over.
Storm managed to scramble up and
raced towards Tom, whinnying loudly.

"Well done, boy!" Tom shouted. "Oh, well done!"

The water gushing from his golden armour, Tom stooped to pick up his fallen sword. Storm was close now, still moving at great speed. Using the power of his leg armour, Tom ran alongside his horse, easily keeping pace with him. He snatched at Storm's reins and swung himself up into the saddle, using the strength given to him by the golden breastplate to mount the stallion at a gallop.

"To Elenna!" he shouted.

Storm turned and reared, neighing loudly. Moments later he was galloping towards the protection of the trees where Elenna and Silver were waiting.

But Trillion was on his feet again, letting out roar after enraged roar. Tom looked back over his shoulder, and saw a deadly light in the lion's fierce green eyes. The evil Beast was getting ready for the kill.

Tom leaned into the wind as Storm raced frantically for the trees.

"Come on!" he called. "Faster, Storm!"

The lion was suddenly horribly close, and Tom could feel his hot, foul breath on his neck. The Beast's jaws snapped, and Storm side-stepped, giving them a few desperate moments while the lion changed direction to keep after them – but it also meant they were heading away from the trees again.

Storm made another sudden change of direction, but Trillion was ready for it this time and his claws slashed through the air, nearly tearing Tom from the saddle. One of the huge heads came terrifyingly close, the open mouth red, the teeth slavering.

Tom kicked out, shouting, "Keep

going, Storm! Don't give up!" But he misjudged the kick, and Trillion's fangs closed around his ankle.

Tom let out a cry of pain as the teeth clamped down and Trillion tried to wrench him from Storm. Tom swung his sword at the Beast, but he was using so much of his strength to stay in the saddle that his blow went wide. Before he could gather himself to strike again, Trillion's teeth bit down even harder on Tom's leg and shook him violently. Tom's fingers were ripped from the reins and he fell with a shout.

He struck the ground hard, only his armour saving him from breaking bones. He lost hold of his sword and shield, but a shred of luck was with him as he rolled over and over, his armour clanking and rattling. His leg was free of Trillion's grasp!

The shooting pains in his ankle were intense. He tried to get to his feet, but his ankle gave way under him and he sprawled breathlessly on the ground.

He could see Elenna and Silver running towards him from the trees.

"No!" he cried. "Go back!" He spotted his sword and shield nearby, and desperately began to crawl over to them.

His fingers were about to close around the hilt of his sword when a massive shape came bounding towards him. Two huge paws crashed down onto the sword and the shield. Tom looked up. Trillion's three heads reared up above him, the six green eyes filled with malice. A blast of stinking breath almost choked Tom as the heads lowered, the drooling jaws ready to rip him to pieces.

The Quest was lost!

CHAPTER EIGHT

THE GOOD BEAST

With a roar, Trillion brought his paw
down hard on Tom's breastplate. Tom
gasped as he felt the weight of the
lion bearing down on him, pressing
him into the ground.

But the golden armour held!

The three heads came closer, a paw
swiping across Tom's face. His helmet

saved him from serious injury, but his visor was up and the points of the monster's claws sliced the skin of his cheek, drawing blood.

The middle head loomed closer, jaws gaping.

Then Tom heard galloping hooves. His horse was coming to the rescue! But Tom knew that Storm was no match for Trillion.

"Go back!" he shouted.

A howl of rage answered him.

Tom twisted around, still pinned to the ground by the evil Beast, and saw with astonishment that it wasn't Storm.

It was *Tagus*!

The horse-man was galloping across the clearing, his sword whirling, as he bore down on the three-headed lion.

Tagus struck Trillion like an avalanche, kicking, bellowing war-cries,

and hacking at the evil Beast with his
sword.

Gasping for breath, Tom managed to
roll clear of the two Beasts. Trillion
was roaring with pain and fury, and
rose up, his claws like knives, lunging

at the horse-man. But Tagus turned in a moment, bringing his hindquarters forwards and lashing out with a powerful double kick that sent Trillion staggering backwards.

Tagus followed up, coming in close, his sword sweeping back and forth as the evil Beast's three heads reared back to avoid the sharp steel.

Then Tom saw what Tagus was

doing. He shouted to Elenna, "He's driving Trillion towards the lake! We have to help!"

Tom got to his feet, ignoring the pain in his ankle as he stumbled to snatch up his sword. He limped forwards, ready to join battle with Tagus. Thrusting his blade, he slashed at the lion's forelegs, helping to force Trillion closer and closer to the water's edge.

"I'm coming!" Tom heard Elenna shout. Out of the corner of his eye, he saw Storm gallop up with Elenna on his back and Silver loping at his side. Elenna leaned far out of the saddle and snatched up Tom's shield, throwing it to him as Storm raced past.

"Thank you!" Tom caught the shield gratefully, but the pain in his ankle was so bad now that he could barely stand.

"I will not give up!" he hissed under his breath, his sword stabbing and cutting at the lion, his shield defending him from the evil Beast's ripping claws. "While there is blood in my veins, I will fight on!"

He shouted to Elenna, trying to lift his voice against the noise of the battling Beasts. "Keep back – all of you! Don't let Storm get too close!" He was not going to risk the horse's life a second time. Also, there was something vitally important that he wanted Elenna and Storm to do. "I've seen the boots!" Tom yelled. "They're lying over there, in the grass!"

"I see them!" Elenna shouted back.

"We'll get them for you!"

Hope filled Tom's heart – but while he was distracted, a paw struck him, knocking him to the ground. Shaking his head, he got to his feet, but the fall had made his injured ankle worse; he could hardly put any weight on it now.

"You're hurt!" Elenna cried. "I'll get you to safety first!"

"No!" Tom shouted, his voice rising above the roaring of the Beasts. "I'm fine – and I won't leave Tagus. Rescue the boots!"

Elenna hesitated, then pulled on Storm's reins, turning the horse. With Silver close behind, she raced towards the boots.

Tom turned again to the desperate battle, hoping he could survive the pain in his ankle long enough to defeat the lion. But with every step towards the lake, Trillion fought more fiercely, and Tagus was beginning to tire.

Suddenly Tom's ankle gave way; he fell to his knees. He needed to be brave like never before. He looked up at Trillion and saw him take another deadly swipe at Tagus. *Enough!* Tom touched his hand against the golden chainmail, which would give him strength of heart. He slowly clambered back to his feet, gritting his teeth as he tried to ignore the pain. Finally, he drew himself up to his full height and raised his sword in the air.

He was ready to end the battle with Trillion.

CHAPTER NINE
NO VICTORY!

The two Beasts were still fighting furiously. The lake was only a short distance away, but driving the three-headed lion back those last few paces was going to take every ounce of strength and courage Tom possessed.

"I'm coming!" he shouted, hobbling forwards, knowing that he was facing a Beast more evil and vicious than any he had encountered before.

Tagus bellowed as his sword struck the lion again and again, but the slashing blade was not able to penetrate the evil Beast's thick hide. With every blow Tom could see that the horse-man was weakening – and the fangs in those three snarling mouths were as sharp and dangerous as ever.

It was now or never! Tom darted towards the lion, coming in behind the three heads, aiming for the huge body. Gripping his sword in both hands, he lunged forwards.

The blade sank deep into the fur and flesh. One of the heads turned angrily and Tom threw himself to the ground as a great paw swung towards his head. His sword-blow had not injured the lion, but merely angered him.

"What kind of Beast is this?" Tom thought. Nothing seemed to hurt him. How could he ever be defeated?

The massive paw struck Tom a glancing blow on the head. He rolled over and over, dizzy and half-stunned. Tagus bellowed and grunted as he struggled to beat the lion back.

Then Tom saw a shape looming above him. He blinked, trying to focus. It was Storm. Elenna was in the saddle and Silver was by their side. Elenna was carrying something that gleamed and shone in the sunlight.

The golden boots!

Tom sat up, his head still spinning.

Elenna leapt from the saddle, holding the boots out. "Put them on!" she said.

Tom reached out, but he was dazed and could barely see straight.

"You'll have to put them on my feet," he gasped. "Quickly! Tagus won't last much longer."

Elenna knelt down and pushed the golden boots onto Tom's feet, taking care with his injured ankle.

Tom sat, panting and giddy, waiting for some sign that the boots would make a difference.

"How do you feel?" Elenna asked anxiously. "Can you stand?"

"No," Tom gasped. Why weren't the boots helping him? Was the Quest going to fail at the final moment?

But then a tingling began to course through him, bringing with it a sensation of strength and power that seemed to flow through his veins. The pain in his ankle faded and suddenly he was clear-headed again.

He sprang to his feet. He felt he could leap over the treetops. This was the power of the golden boots! Gripping his sword and shield he ran towards the battling Beasts. Trillion's last moment had come. Nothing could save the lion now.

Tom lifted his sword, ready to deliver the final blow. But a few paces away from Trillion, he was brought to a halt by an invisible force. He staggered back, then ran forwards once more. Again the invisible wall repelled him. He could not get to the evil Beast.

What was happening?

A black whirlwind appeared close to the water's edge. The air was shrill with the howling wind, but then the darkness was gone – and Malvel was standing at the lakeside.

The Dark Wizard was keeping Tom from the monster! Tom beat at the invisible wall with his sword, but he could not get through.

"I warn you, boy – if you achieve

victory here you will regret it!" Malvel
called. "It will take you to places you
would not choose to visit."

Tom felt the power of Avantia blazing
in him. "I don't care!" he shouted,
hacking at the wall. "I will defeat you,
Malvel – whatever the price!"

"Such arrogance in one so young!"
Malvel cried.

He made a wide gesture with his
arm and suddenly an image
of Aduro appeared. Tom
gasped. The good
wizard was lying on
the ground, beaten
and bloodied.

Behind Malvel's
invisible barrier,
Tagus and Trillion
were still fighting
furiously. Silver was

scrabbling against the barrier, howling with anger and frustration. Elenna was firing arrows from Storm's back, but they bounced uselessly off the magical force field.

"I warn you one last time," cried Malvel. "If you defeat Trillion, I will make you pay in ways that you cannot imagine!"

Tom let his sword-arm fall as he stared at the image of his good friend. Aduro was a powerful wizard, and yet Malvel had crushed him. How could Tom hope to stand against such evil strength?

CHAPTER TEN

THE LION GATE

A triumphant roar from Trillion made Tom turn away from the Dark Wizard. Tagus was falling back, his strength failing. The great lion was overpowering him. The battle would soon be lost.

"Remember my words!" Malvel's mocking voice called.

"I shall," Tom shouted defiantly. "But they won't stop me!"

His sword wasn't able to break through the invisible wall, but he felt more power rising up through his body, power that was coming from the golden boots. Could they destroy the magical barrier?

He brought one foot back and then let fly with a powerful kick. There was a noise so loud that it sounded like the sky shattering. Malvel let out a howl of rage. The invisible barrier was gone!

Tom ran forwards. But suddenly both his sword and shield flew from his grip. Malvel was stopping at nothing!

"Tom – no! Get back!" Elenna called. "You'll be killed."

"I don't need any weapons," Tom shouted, his whole body tingling

with energy. "My armour gives me all the strength I need!"

Tagus was down, still swinging with his sword, as the evil Beast loomed over him. Tom leapt at the lion, grabbing one of his manes. Digging his heels into Trillion's shoulders, he heaved backwards.

Trillion stumbled to one side, taken unawares by Tom's assault, but turned his head quickly, the jaws opening. Undaunted, Tom thrust his arm into the lion's mouth. The golden armour held! Tom saw the lion's teeth splintering into shards.

With a roar of agony, the head reared back, blood dripping from its foaming lips, and the lion dropped back onto his haunches. All three heads pulled away from Tom, the six green eyes filled with pain, and one of Trillion's huge paws shot towards him, the claws unsheathed. Tom knocked the paw aside with a single blow of his fist. Again, Trillion roared and his eyes glittered with a vicious light. Rearing up, he prepared to bring all his mighty weight down on Tom and crush him to the ground.

But as Trillion lifted himself onto his hind legs, Tom saw his opportunity. Instead of running away from the Beast, he lunged forwards, his arms up above his head, pushing against Trillion's underbelly. The armour had made him so powerful that he was able to force the lion backwards.

"I'm stronger than you now!" Tom shouted. "You've failed!"

Roaring and snarling, Trillion fell back, his claws useless, his three sets of teeth biting at the air. Tom pushed again and again, driving the Beast closer to the lake. He had never been so determined.

Too late, the evil Beast realised his peril. Trillion tried to writhe away and avoid the water, but Tom was merciless. With a final mighty shove, he sent the lion plunging into the lake.

The water foamed as the Beast
thrashed helplessly. But the more
Trillion struggled, the deeper he sank,
his thick fur becoming waterlogged,
and his great manes dragging him
further down.

Tom stood at the water's edge,

unable to tear his eyes away from the dreadful sight as the lion fought to keep afloat. There was terror and fury in the six green eyes as the waters closed over the three heads. A paw broke the surface for a moment, and then Trillion could be seen no more. Bubbles boiled and there was a strange hush. The roaring of the three-headed lion was silenced for ever.

Elenna stood at Tom's side. She rested her hand on his shoulder.

"You did it," she said quietly. "You defeated the most powerful Beast Malvel has ever sent!"

But Tom frowned. All the evil Beasts he had fought in his Quest for the golden armour had dissolved into small versions of themselves after he had beaten them. He was expecting the same to happen with Trillion. But the lake's surface was clear and smooth. He looked at Elenna. "There aren't any little lions," he said. "Why do you think that is?"

"I don't know," Elenna said. "Perhaps…"

Her words were interrupted by a low rumbling sound that made the ground tremble under their feet. The surface of the lake began to shiver. Ripples spread from the place where Trillion had last been seen. The water surged and heaved, and a deep growl shook the air.

Then the waters parted as a vast domed shape rose majestically out of the lake, black as ebony, running with water and shining darkly in the sun. It towered above the two friends, shedding rivers of lake water.

A statue of a huge lion's head stood
before them, its jaws wide open.
A causeway had formed between it
and the shore, and a path led
through the enormous teeth.

"It's a gateway," Tom murmured in awe.

"Leading where?" Elenna wondered.

"I don't know," Tom replied. "But I have to follow the path. Something is drawing me forwards."

"It could be dangerous," Elenna warned. "Malvel may have created it."

Tom looked back. The Dark Wizard had vanished. "That doesn't matter," he said. He took his magical compass from his pocket and held it out in front of him. It had been left to him by his father, Taladon, and had already saved his life. The needle pointed to *Destiny*.

A powerful certainty filled Tom. "I know where Malvel has gone," he said. He pointed to the open jaws. "He's beyond the gateway. And I think Aduro is there, too." He looked at Elenna. "I have to go."

"You mean *we* have to go," Elenna corrected him.

Tom turned and saw that Storm and Silver were right behind them. Not for the first time, he was grateful to have such loyal friends.

Tom took Storm's reins and strode out onto the causeway, his horse following fearlessly. Elenna walked at his shoulder, her hand in Silver's grey fur as he paced alongside her.

The air shimmered all around the lion's jaws, tingling on Tom's skin and making his hair stand on end. As the four companions paused before the gaping fangs, Tom's golden armour glowed in the sunlight.

He and Elenna exchanged glances.

"Ready?" Tom asked.

"Ready," Elenna reassured him.

Then the four friends walked into the lion's gate, following the path that would lead them to their next adventure.

Tom had a destiny to fulfil. The Beast Quest was far from over.

JOIN TOM ON HIS NEXT
BEAST QUEST SOON!

Look out for Series 3

THE DARK REALM

Can Tom free the good
Beasts from the
Dark Realm?

Fight the Beasts,
Fear the Magic

www.beastquest.co.uk

Have you checked out the all-new Beast Quest website?
It's the place to go for games, downloads, activities,
sneak previews and lots of fun!

You can read all about your favourite Beast Quest
monsters, download free screensavers and desktop
wallpapers for your computer, and send
beastly e-cards to your friends.

Sign up to the newsletter at www.beastquest.co.uk
to receive exclusive extra content and the opportunity
to enter special members-only competitions. It's the best
place to go for up-to-date info on all the Beast Quest
books, including the next exciting series,
which features six brand new Beasts.

Win an exclusive
Beast Quest T-shirt and goody bag!

Tom has battled many fearsome Beasts and we want to know
which one is your favourite! Send us a drawing or painting of
your favourite Beast and tell us in 30 words why you think
it's the best.

Each month we will select **three** winners to receive
a Beast Quest T-shirt and goody bag!

Send your entry on a postcard to
BEAST QUEST COMPETITION
Orchard Books, 338 Euston Road, London NW1 3BH.

Australian readers should email:
childrens.books@hachette.com.au

New Zealand readers should write to:
Beast Quest Competition, 4 Whetu Place, Mairangi Bay,
Auckland NZ, or email: childrensbooks@hachette.co.nz

**Don't forget to include your name and address.
Only one entry per child.**

Good luck!

by Adam Blade

Series 1

Series 2: The Golden Armour

All priced at £4.99
Vedra & Krimon: Twin Beasts of Avantia is priced at £5.99

The Beast Quest books are available from all good
bookshops, or can be ordered direct from the publisher:
Orchard Books, PO BOX 29, Douglas IM99 1BQ.
Credit card orders please telephone 01624 836000
or fax 01624 837033 or visit our website: www.orchardbooks.co.uk
or e-mail: bookshop@enterprise.net for details.

To order please quote title, author
and ISBN and your full name and address.
Cheques and postal orders should be made payable to 'Bookpost plc.'
Postage and packing is FREE within the UK
(overseas customers should add £2.00 per book).

Prices and availability are subject to change.